GHOST DETECTORS

Beware the Headless Horseman!

BOOK 11

BY

DOTTI ENDERLE

ILLUSTRATED BY

HOWARD MCWILLIAM

magic wagon

visit us at www.abdopublishing.com

A big thank you to Adrienne Enderle — DE
With thanks to my ever-supportive wife Rebecca — HM

Published by Magic Wagon, a division of the ABDO Group,
8000 West 78th Street, Edina, Minnesota 55439. Copyright
© 2012 by Abdo Consulting Group, Inc. International copyrights
reserved in all countries. All rights reserved. No part of this
book may be reproduced in any form without written permission
from the publisher.

Calico Chapter Books™ is a trademark and logo of Magic Wagon.

Printed in the United States of America, North Mankato, Minnesota
052011
102012

 This book contains at least 10% recycled materials.

Text by Dotti Enderle
Illustrations by Howard McWilliam
Edited by Stephanie Hedlund and Rochelle Baltzer
Cover and interior design by Jaime Martens

Library of Congress Cataloging-in-Publication Data

Enderle, Dotti, 1954-
  Beware the headless horseman! / by Dotti Enderle ; illustrated by
Howard McWilliam.
       p. cm. -- (Ghost Detectors ; bk. 11)
   ISBN 978-1-61641-627-0
   [1. Horses--Fiction. 2. Ghosts--Fiction. 3. Humorous stories.] I.
McWilliam, Howard, 1977- ill. II. Title.
   PZ7.E69645Be 2011
   [Fic]--dc22
                                              2011001844

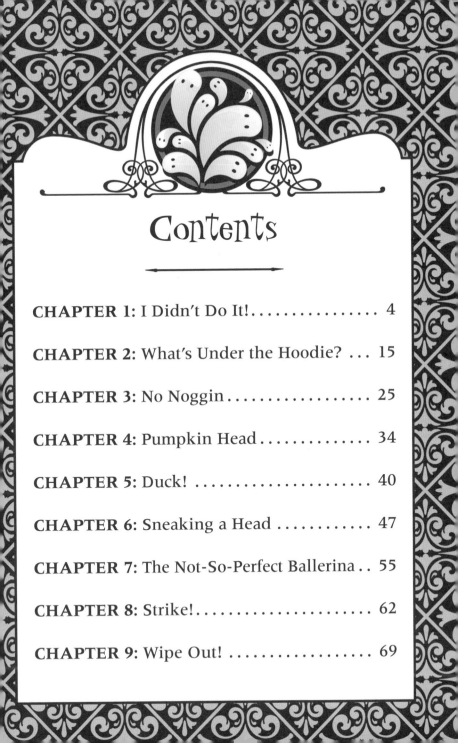

Contents

I Didn't Do It!

Malcolm hopped on his bike and met his best friend, Dandy, at the corner of their street.

"What's the emergency?" Dandy asked.

Dandy had gotten a new bike for his birthday—a bike about three inches too tall. He tried to keep one foot on the ground and his bottom on the seat as he struggled to stay upright.

"It's not really an emergency," Malcolm said. "Mr. Gable called and asked us to come over. He sounded desperate."

Dandy's face turned a bright shade of turnip. "Mr. Gable . . . the guy who owns the horse stables?"

"Yeah, him," Malcolm answered.

Dandy's face went from turnip to eggplant. "I didn't do it!"

"Didn't do what?" Malcolm asked. Usually when Dandy denied something, it was probably because he *did* do it.

"Maybe you should go alone," Dandy said, trying to maneuver his bike around.

"Didn't do *what*?" Malcolm urged.

"It was nothing," Dandy said.

"Dandy, what didn't you do?"

Dandy let out a guilty sigh. "I *did* go visit the stables a couple of weeks ago."

"Yeah . . . ," Malcolm encouraged.

"And I *did* feed Lulu—the squatty gray horse—a carrot."

"And?" Malcolm egged.

"And I *did* accidentally open the gate."

Malcolm scratched his head. "So what was it that you didn't do?"

"I didn't invite Lulu to follow me home," Dandy said, shifting the weight of his bike to keep it upright.

"A horse followed you home? That's crazy!"

"It was more than crazy," Dandy said. "Around dinnertime my mom looked out the window and saw a horse on the back porch chomping on her geraniums. She

was going to call Mr. Gable to come pick Lulu up, but I offered to lead her back home.

"Since I couldn't use my bike, it took me one hour and four carrots to get her back to the stable. I don't think Mr. Gable saw us, but maybe he did. I'm in big trouble!"

"If you were in trouble," Malcolm said, "Mr. Gable would've called you, not me."

Dandy's bottom slipped off the seat. He scooched back on. "Did he say what he wanted?"

Malcolm shrugged. "Nope. He just said that it was important."

"I'm right behind you," Dandy said.

Malcolm pushed off on his bike, turned the corner, and made it to the next block before noticing that Dandy was not right

behind him. Where was he? Malcolm circled back to find Dandy trying to balance the bike and take off.

"You should use the fire hydrant," Malcolm suggested.

Dandy walked the bike to the nearest fire hydrant, put his foot on the spout, then boosted himself onto his bike. It was a wobbly start, but he finally got his balance. He and Malcolm rode on to the stables.

The smell of cut grass and green hay met them as they neared the pasture. They rode by a long wooden fence until they reached the large double gates. The sign just above read: *Gable Stables and Horse Farm.*

Malcolm hopped off his bike and entered the gate. Dandy fell off his bike, then crept in behind Malcolm.

"Come on," Malcolm said. "You're not in trouble."

That's when Mr. Gable rushed out of the barn toward them. "You!" he shouted, lumbering their way.

"I didn't do it! I didn't do it!" Dandy cried.

Mr. Gable scratched his head. "Didn't do what?"

Dandy pretended to adjust his bike. "Uh . . . nothing."

"I'm just so glad you boys are here," Mr. Gable said. "It's been horrible."

Malcolm looked around at the beautiful setting. There was a large red barn, a full green pasture, and horses prancing in a gated arena. What could be so horrible?

"What's wrong?" Malcolm asked.

Mr. Gable shifted his eyes left and right, like he was worried someone might overhear. It seemed kind of silly since no one else was around, unless you counted the grasshopper that was perched on a stem of grass.

"Is it true what I hear about you two?" Mr. Gable said.

Dandy turned all turnipy with panic again. "What'd you hear?"

"You know," Mr. Gable said, nodding like they should know.

Malcolm waited, then said, "I'm not sure what you mean."

Mr. Gable leaned in and whispered, "I heard you boys have gotten rid of a ghost or two around town."

Whoa! Malcolm took a step back. Dandy tripped over his bike. *Mr. Gable knew?*

Malcolm and Dandy had done a lot of ghost hunting since Malcolm got his Ecto-Handheld-Automatic-Heat-Sensitive-Laser-Enhanced Specter Detector. But he thought their ghostly adventures were mostly a secret.

"Yeah," Malcolm admitted. "We've got the equipment and the expertise."

Malcolm swelled with pride. Then he thought, *Hmmm . . . Maybe I should start my own ghost-hunting agency! Wouldn't that be great? I could even have some business cards made.*

Mr. Gable wrung his jittery hands as he spoke. "I've got a ghost here, and it's a doozy."

"Define doozy," Dandy said, fumbling to pick up his bike.

"Like I've never seen before," Mr. Gable proclaimed.

"You've actually seen it?" Malcolm asked.

"Not so much seen it as heard it," he whispered. "He gallops through the fields, spooking the horses."

Dandy's face was covered in confusion. "The ghost is a horse?"

"No," Mr. Gable corrected. "Well, partly. It's a rider on a phantom steed. I hear the hooves beating the ground as he rides by. And even though it's a ghost, the

pounding of those hooves stir up a cloud of dust. Makes me sneeze every time."

Malcolm had never tackled a ghost on horseback before. This could be a challenge.

"So you want us to—" Malcolm began.

"Whatever it is you do," Mr. Gable finished. "I need that ghost gone. It's bad for business."

"We'll do what we can," Malcolm assured him.

"Can you do it now?" Mr. Gable asked. "The sooner he's gone, the better."

"I'll have to go home and grab my equipment," Malcolm told him. "Then we'll get right to work."

Malcolm proudly pushed off on his bike, ready for business. Of course he had to wait on Dandy to gain enough leverage to get on.

What's Under the Hoodie?

Malcolm wound around the gate, then skidded to a stop.

Dandy, who'd just gotten some momentum, slammed right into him. "Ouch! Why'd you stop?"

"Because I was thinking that maybe you should wait here," Malcolm suggested.

"You're going to leave me here with a galloping ghost?"

"Just for a few minutes," Malcolm said. "I think I can go faster on my own."

Dandy pouted. "My new bike is fast. I could outride you."

Malcolm didn't doubt that. Dandy's new bike was sweet! But it's hard to ride like the wind when you can barely reach the pedals. "Look, just hang back. I won't be long."

"Okay," Dandy said. "I'll be on the lookout for anything suspicious."

"Good idea." Malcolm pushed off and pumped with fury, heading home to grab his ghost-detecting gizmos.

Just ten minutes later, Malcolm returned. Dandy's bike was leaning against the fence, but no Dandy. *Huh? Where is he? Could he have been trampled by the phantom rider?* Maybe Malcolm shouldn't have left him alone.

But as Malcolm got closer, he saw Dandy standing on the railings by the barn. He was feeding carrots to a very grateful Lulu. *Probably not a good idea,* Malcolm thought.

"Hey, look!" Dandy said, placing a carrot in his mouth. Lulu reached over with her big horsey teeth and ... *chomp!* "She loves me," Dandy beamed, chewing the bit of carrot left between his lips.

"Cool," Malcolm said. "But it's time to leave your girlfriend behind. We've got a ghost to zap."

"She's not my girlfriend," Dandy argued. "We just like sharing a meal."

Dandy hopped off the railing and joined Malcolm, who was unzipping his backpack.

Mr. Gable rushed over. "You're back," he said, fidgety. "Can you get started?

The sooner that thing's gone, the sooner I can sleep without a night-light."

Malcolm powered up his specter detector. "Stand back."

But Mr. Gable didn't take a step back. He took a clumsy step forward instead. "Is that a blower dryer?"

"No," Malcolm said. "I'm here to catch a ghost, not style its hair."

"Well, it looks like a blow dryer," Mr. Gable stated.

"Well, it's not," Malcolm countered. "Now, if you'll excuse us—"

"—we have a job to do," Dandy finished. Lulu reached over the rails and gave Dandy a long, sloppy lick on the face.

"Not your girlfriend, huh?" Malcolm muttered.

"Let's go find the ghost," Dandy said, stomping off. "I don't want to be late for dinner."

They left Mr. Gable standing near the stables and slinked around to the back pasture.

"Be careful!" Malcolm warned, jerking Dandy back.

"Is it the ghost?" Dandy cried.

Malcolm shook his head. "No. I mean be careful where you step." He pointed down at a pile of dried horse droppings.

"Oh, yeah. Thanks," Dandy said, tiptoeing around it.

Malcolm handed the ghost zapper to Dandy. "If he's here, we'll have to be quick. Keep your finger on that button and be ready to spray him."

"Will I have to spray the horse, too?" Dandy asked.

"Let's get the rider first."

Malcolm looked out at the deep, rolling pasture. Would they have to trek the whole field or would the phantom horseman charge close by? There was no point waiting.

"This way," Malcolm said, pointing to a clump of trees in the distance.

"I don't want to go out too far," Dandy said. "There might be chiggers."

Malcolm hadn't thought of that. "Good point. Let's stay out of the tall grass."

They crept slowly, as though the ghost might be hiding in a patch of brush.

"Why can't we see him?" Dandy asked. "Is the specter detector on?"

Malcolm checked the green button and listened for the hum. "It's on."

"Maybe the ghost rider is napping," Dandy suggested.

"Or maybe one of Mr. Gable's horses got loose and he thought it was a ghost," Malcolm said. "He is the jumpy type."

A chill rolled down Malcolm's neck. "Dandy, did you feel that?"

The frozen expression on Dandy's face said yes.

They both turned slowly . . . slowly . . . slowly . . . *Ahhhh!!!*

A large black steed had snuck up behind them. It reared back, hoofing the air above their heads. The boys stumbled back, getting out of the way of the giant stallion.

"What do I do?" Dandy asked, the zapper wobbling in his hands.

"Zap it!" Malcolm shouted.

"The horse?" Dandy cried.

Then, before Malcolm could answer, the horse dropped its hooves to the ground and revealed its rider. Malcolm and Dandy froze, too stunned to move.

Mounted upon the horse was a man wearing gray boots, jeans, and a gray hoodie. Any other day that might look normal. Except there was no face peeking out from the hoodie. None. Then the rider threw back the hood of his shirt and . . . There was no face! And even worse, there was no head!

Yikes!

"What are you waiting for?" Malcolm said.

But Dandy flubbed and fumbled the zapper as the ghost rode off.

"Get him!" Malcolm shouted.

They raced behind the horse, watching it put a good distance between them.

"How far will this thing spray?" Dandy asked.

Malcolm stopped. "Not that far," he sighed.

The rider turned toward them, waved good-bye, and vanished among the trees.

"I can't believe we missed him," Malcolm said, feeling deflated.

"He took us by surprise," Dandy said. "We'll be ready for him next time."

"Yeah," Malcolm agreed. "And now we know to aim for his belly."

No Noggin

"Did you see him?" Mr. Gable asked as they trudged back to the barn.

"Not exactly," Malcolm said.

Mr. Gable fidgeted. "What'd he look like?"

Malcolm looked at Dandy. Dandy looked at Malcolm. Neither knew exactly what to say.

"We . . . uh . . . didn't see his face," Dandy hemmed and hawed.

"Had his back to you, heh?" Mr. Gable asked.

"No," Malcolm said. "He was facing us. Sort of. It's just that, he didn't have a face."

Mr. Gable stopped fidgeting. His eye twitched. "No face?"

"It's worse than that," Malcolm said. "He didn't have a head."

"No head? Oh no!" Mr. Gable moaned, clutching his heart. "A headless horseman?" Mr. Gable paced back and forth. "Oh my. Oh dear. I was afraid of this."

"Afraid of what?" Malcolm asked.

"Afraid he'd come back," Mr. Gable mumbled, still pacing, pacing, pacing.

"Who?" Malcolm urged. "Who'd come back?"

Mr. Gable stopped dead still. He glanced over his right shoulder, then his left. Then, he leaned so close Malcolm could smell egg salad on his breath.

"Bailey Winsome," he whispered.

Malcolm and Dandy glanced at each other again. It was up to one of them to ask the obvious question. Dandy finally asked, "Who's Bailey Winsome?"

"Shhhhh!" Mr. Gable paced again. "He was my hired hand. Used to train the horses. He worked here about nine years, give or take. Best trainer I've ever had."

"What happened to him?" Malcolm asked.

Mr. Gable stopped to explain. "He got cocky. He'd prance around on the horses doing all manner of tricks and stunts. He liked to show off."

"Sounds kinda cool," Dandy said.

Mr. Gable nodded. "It was at first. But pretty soon he started neglecting his other duties. He decided he could make more money doing his tricks at a circus. He asked me to loan him a horse."

"I'm guessing you didn't," Malcolm said.

"You guessed right. Some of those tricks were dangerous. I couldn't risk one of my horses getting hurt."

Dandy's eyes lit up with curiosity. "What kind of tricks could he do?"

Mr. Gable shrugged. "Stupid tricks like jumping through a big ring of fire. Skating along beside the horse as it raced over a bed of hot coals. And dressing himself and the horse in matching tutus and doing pirouettes to Swan Lake."

Mr. Gable paused. "Okay, that last one wasn't so much dangerous as humiliating. But I couldn't stand for it."

"He must've been pretty mad," Malcolm said.

"Madder than a horse in a tutu," Mr. Gable told him. He began pacing again.

"So what happened to him?" Dandy asked.

Mr. Gable did another quick look over his shoulders. "That's the tragic part. He got more and more reckless. I never saw that boy sitting proper on a horse after that. He was either standing on his head or holding on underneath. I don't think the horses much liked it, but he didn't care. He just rode any which way he pleased.

"Then about a month ago, he was riding Bullet. That horse is faster than a locomotive

in a mudslide. Bailey raced him through the pasture. Bullet was kicking it at maximum speed. They came charging by me so fast I could hear the wind whistling off them as they whizzed by.

"I called out to Bailey, ordering him to stop. But just as I yelled, he sat up and looked back. He never saw that tree branch. It knocked his head clean off."

Malcolm didn't know what to say. He just stood with his mouth gaping. Dandy looked just as flabbergasted. He gulped twice then asked, "Is that possible?"

Mr. Gable raised an eyebrow. "Did I mention Bullet is fast?"

"So why do you think he's haunting your stables?" Malcolm asked.

Mr. Gable paced as he spoke. "Could be that he's rode these pastures so often it's like second nature to him."

That could be it, but Malcolm didn't think so.

"Could be that he blames me for losing his noggin," Mr. Gable continued.

That's it. Why else would Bailey Winsome's ghost strike terror in this man?

"So he's done all kinds of things to hurt you, right?" Malcolm asked him. "Like slamming your fingers in the door? Filling your boots with sharp rocks? Switching your ketchup with hot sauce?"

Mr. Gable scratched his head. "None of that."

"Hmmmm," Malcolm pondered. "Any other reason he'd be hanging around?"

"Could be," Mr. Gable added in a whisper, "he's looking for his head."

Malcolm and Dandy gave each other a questioning look. "Uh, what happened to

the one that got knocked off?" Malcolm asked.

"Well, I guess that's my fault, too," Mr. Gable admitted. "When I went inside to call 9-1-1, a wake of buzzards winged in, picked it up by the hair, and carried it off. Nobody's seen it since."

Malcolm had never tackled a job like this before. How do you face a ghost with no face?

"It's going to be hard to zap him," Malcolm said, thinking about their encounter in the pasture. "We'll have to try other measures."

"What other measures?" Dandy asked.

"A peace offering," Malcolm explained. "We'll give him what he wants."

Dandy gulped. "Wouldn't it be easier to stretch out on top of the barn, then when he rides by – *zap!* – gotcha!"

"No, I think he's too smart for that," Malcolm said.

"Too smart?" Dandy argued. "He doesn't have a head. That means he doesn't have a brain. How smart can he be?"

"Smart enough to spook the horses, terrorize Mr. Gable, and outsmart us," Malcolm told him.

Mr. Gable paced. "I am terrorized," he admitted.

"That's it then," Malcolm decided. "We're going with the new plan. We're going to give Bailey a brand-new head."

Pumpkin Head

They rode back to Malcolm's house, Malcolm zipping along, Dandy standing on tiptoes to pedal. He'd gained some pretty good momentum until they came to the stop sign. He grabbed the sign pole to stay upright until they could cross the street.

Once they got inside, Dandy asked, "Now what?"

"We've got to find a way to give Bailey his head back," Malcolm answered.

Dandy made a sour face. "Ew! Even if we could find it, don't you think it'd be kind of . . . uh . . . "

"Not his real head," Malcolm said. "A substitute head. Something he can balance on his shoulders and be proud of."

Dandy's face lit up like he finally understood. "You mean something big and round."

"Exactly!"

"Like what?" Dandy asked, scratching his head and looking around the room.

"I'm not sure yet," Malcolm said, "but I've got an idea." He walked over to the bookcase and skimmed the titles. The top shelf held his collection of ghost stories. He selected one in particular—*The Legend of Sleepy Hollow* by Washington Irving.

"Oh yeah, I know that story," Dandy said. "It's about the Headless Horseman."

"Yep." Malcolm thumbed through the pages. "Here," he said, showing Dandy an illustration of the horseman crossing a bridge. "He's got a pumpkin."

"A pumpkin?" Dandy studied the drawing like he might be asked to copy it.

"Why not? It worked for the original Headless Horseman," Malcolm said. "It could work now."

"Let's try it!" Dandy said.

Malcolm paused, closing the book. "There's only one problem."

"Just one?" Dandy asked.

"Okay, there's one big problem," Malcolm corrected. "Where are we going to find a pumpkin? I only see them at

Halloween. Where do you find pumpkins in months that don't start with an *O*?"

They both sat down, staring at the ceiling and pondering what to do. Then Malcolm got an idea. "Up there," he said, pointing to the ceiling.

Dandy twisted his head left and right, trying to see what Malcolm was talking about. "Up where?"

"Up there . . . in the attic."

They hopped up and dashed into the hallway. Malcolm pulled the cord, lowering the attic door. Then he unfolded the ladder that led up.

"You have a pumpkin up there?" Dandy asked, brushing the dust from his nose.

Malcolm led Dandy up the ladder. He went right to a box labeled Halloween

and popped it open. "There may be more than one."

He was right. There were three pumpkins inside the box. Malcolm pulled out the biggest—a heavy ceramic cookie jar with a jack-o'-lantern face. Its expression looked more like a clown than a Halloween spook.

"This should do it," Malcolm said with pride. "Let's go."

"But it's not like a real head," Dandy pointed out. "It has a lid."

Malcolm shrugged. "Maybe he'll think it's a hat."

They hurried out to grab their bikes, but when they opened the door – *Wheeeeeeee!* – they were met with a blast of steamy hot breath. Lulu had followed them home!

The horse bobbed her head, stuck out her scratchy tongue, and – *sluuuurrrrppp* – gave Dandy a big ookey kiss.

"Your girlfriend found you," Malcolm teased.

"She's not my girlfriend," Dandy argued, wiping horse spit off his cheek.

Malcolm laughed. "We'll tie her to your bike and take her back with us."

Duck!

Malcolm fastened several of his sister's belts together and slipped a loop around Lulu's neck. The trek to Gable Stables took three times as long since they had to walk their bikes back.

"Okay," Malcolm said as they approached the horse farm, "you sneak Lulu back to the barn. I'll slip around back and power up the specter detector. Once we give Bailey his new head, we'll all be happy."

"Easy peasy?" Dandy asked.

"Yep. Mr. Gable might even give us a reward."

"That'd be great," Dandy said, leading Lulu away.

Malcolm dropped his backpack, then— *Oops! Did he just smash the cookie jar into pumpkin slices?* He unzipped the pack and it came out in one piece (or two if you counted the lid).

"Done!" Dandy said, slipping up behind Malcolm.

Malcolm fumbled with the cookie jar, but thankfully didn't drop it. "Don't sneak up behind me like that." That made two near misses on cracking Bailey's new head.

Dandy sat down next to him. "Sorry," he apologized.

Malcolm powered up the specter detector. "He's got to be around here somewhere," he said, searching the pasture.

A breeze blew across the field, and within moments, Bailey Winsome blew in with it.

"There he is!" Dandy whispered. "What are we going to do?"

Malcolm didn't answer. He couldn't believe it! Bailey rode toward them with his shoulders balancing on his horse's back. His legs were sticking up, forming a giant *V*.

"He's riding upside-down," Dandy said.

"He's doing more than that," Malcolm pointed out.

Bailey crossed his legs, forming an *X*. Then back to a *V*. Then an *X*. On and on.

"It's a scissor trick!" Dandy shouted. "Boy, he sure is flexible."

Malcolm did an eye roll. "He's a ghost, Dandy. All ghosts are flexible."

"Bet they can't all do that," Dandy said, pointing.

Bailey had gone from scissoring to spinning. He twirled like a cyclone as his horse pranced about.

"That's pretty good," Dandy called out, clapping his hands.

"Shhh!" Malcolm warned.

Too late. Bailey had stopped his performance and was trotting their way. Malcolm inched toward him, holding out the pumpkin jar.

Bailey waited, his phantom horse pawing the earth.

Then, when they were dangerously close to him, Malcolm tossed the cookie jar up to Bailey. Bailey caught it with one hand, causing the lid to rattle. He twisted his hand this way and that, checking it over.

"See?" Malcolm said. "We brought you a new head."

"With a hat," Dandy added.

"It even has a nice face," Malcolm said.

Dandy nodded. "Perfect for the circus."

Bailey held the jar up. Malcolm was sure he'd try it on for size. But rather than rest it on his shoulders, he reared back and—"

"Run, Dandy!"

They both shot across the field as quick as they could. Bailey spurred his horse into a gallop and chased them.

Malcolm and Dandy sprinted for their lives, arms swinging. Malcolm ventured a peek over his shoulders. Bailey was standing on the horse, arms spread airplane-style. He had one leg out behind him as he balanced on the other. He still held the cookie jar in his right hand.

Bailey planted both feet on the horse's back, pulled the pumpkin close, and then did a wind-up like a baseball pitcher.

Malcolm knew what was coming next. "Dandy, duck!"

Bailey threw the ceramic pumpkin. Malcolm and Dandy dove into the grass just as the cookie jar sailed over their heads and crashed into the side of the barn.

Bailey circled back, made a sweeping bow, and disappeared.

Malcolm's plan had failed.

"This stinks!" Malcolm said, spitting grass out of his mouth.

Dandy rolled over. "No, this stinks." He'd missed getting smashed with a cookie jar, but he hadn't missed the gigantic pile of horse droppings. "Why do these things always happen to me?"

Sneaking a Head

"What now?" Dandy asked after he'd taken a shower, changed clothes, and dumped half a bottle of his dad's menthol aftershave on his neck and hands.

Malcolm sat a little farther away now that Dandy smelled like his Grandma Eunice's arthritis cream. "Now we come up with a new plan."

Dandy sniffed his T-shirt. "I don't understand why the pumpkin didn't

work. Didn't the Headless Horseman in Sleepy Hollow wear his?"

"Uh . . .," Malcolm stuttered. "Not really."

Dandy's mouth twitched. "Then why'd he have it?"

Malcolm hesitated. "He, uh, threw it at someone."

"Oh great," Dandy complained. "We should've known a pumpkin wouldn't work. So what do we do now?"

Malcolm leaned forward, hugging his knees. "We find something that does work."

"Zapping works," Dandy said.

Malcolm shook his head. "It only works if we can catch him. We can't. That horse is too fast." He thought a moment. "We'll just have to find another head."

Dandy sniffed his underarms. "Like what?"

Malcolm didn't answer. His wheels were cranking. Then he smiled. "I've got it. Follow me."

They slipped into the hallway and toward Grandma Eunice's bedroom.

"Why are we going in there?" Dandy asked.

Malcolm put a finger to his lips. "Shhhh!"

They tiptoed like spies, creeping closer and closer. Malcolm peeked through the doorway. There sat Grandma Eunice, snoozing in her wheelchair.

Malcolm motioned Dandy forward, then he pointed across the room. On a dresser by the bed stood a Styrofoam head wearing a wiry, electric-blue wig.

Dandy nodded.

They softly crept in, when suddenly, *snort-snort-snort-snort-snort!*

They froze, then relaxed. Grandma snored like a bulldozer.

Then when they were halfway across the room, *Yum! Yum! Yum! Yum! Yum!*

Dandy gave Malcolm a puzzled look.

"She's dreaming about carrot cake," Malcolm whispered.

Dandy breathed a sigh of relief.

They finally reached their destination. Malcolm carefully picked up the wig head and they tiptoed back to the door. Just as they were about to exit, Grandma lifted her head.

"Plan on wearing that for picture day?" she asked.

Malcolm felt pretty stupid standing there holding the wig. "Uh . . . uh . . ."

Grandma rolled over to the dresser and tossed Malcolm a hairbrush. "Gussy it up real pretty," she cackled. Then added, "You didn't have to sneak it out of here. You could've just asked me. I've been meaning to get rid of that thing anyway. It makes my scalp itch."

Malcolm grinned and said, "Thanks, Grandma."

She dropped her head again and within seconds, *snort-snort-snort-snort-snort!*

"Now," Malcolm said as they hurried down into his basement lab, "let's grab the tools and get back over to Gable Stables."

Dandy smelled his arm. "This wig head seems so . . . faceless."

It was true. There was curves and dents shaped like two eyes and a mouth, but there were no colors filling them in.

"That's easily fixed," Malcolm said. He reached in a drawer and pulled out a box of markers. "Now, what color eyes do you think Bailey would like?"

"What color do you think they were before?"

Malcolm shrugged. "Who knows. But let's give him blue eyes just in case."

Malcolm dug out a marker labeled *Denim*. He colored in the eyes, careful to stay in the lines.

"I've never seen anyone with eyes that color," Dandy observed. "Sort of looks like my dad's blue jean jacket."

"Oh well," Malcolm said, dotting in some black pupils. He used the same black on the nostrils. "What about the mouth? Pink?"

They scrambled through the box.

"Who knew there were so many shades of the same color?" Dandy said, holding up a marker labeled *Shocking Pink*.

Malcolm grimaced. "Ew. Put that down. It reminds me of my sister's loud mouth." He continued to pick through the

markers until he found the perfect shade, Tea Rose.

"Kinda girly, isn't it?" Dandy asked.

"It'll match his tutu," Malcolm teased.

Once the process was done, it did look like a girl. "I don't think he'll mind," Malcolm said. "It's better than a jack-o'-lantern."

They grabbed their things and headed up the stairs. Dandy lifted the bottom of his shirt and sniffed.

"Why do you keep doing that?" Malcolm asked.

"'Cause I want to make sure I don't smell like apples," Dandy answered.

Malcolm grinned. "Think of it as a gift from your girlfriend, Lulu."

Dandy stamped his foot. "She's not my girlfriend!"

The Not-So-Perfect Ballerina

Mr. Gable met them at the gate. "Is he gone yet?"

"Not yet," Malcolm told him. "But we'll get him this time." He held up the head with the crazy wig.

Mr. Gable twitched. "That's about the ugliest thing I've ever seen."

"Uglier than no head?" Dandy asked.

"Well . . .," Mr. Gable said, thinking about it. "Yes."

"Let's see if it works anyway," Malcolm said.

Mr. Gable scooted back to his house while Malcolm and Dandy cruised around back.

Malcolm switched on the specter detector. "Hey, Bailey! We've got another present for you! You'll like this one."

No sooner had he spoken when Bailey appeared, mounted on his horse. He towered just a few feet from them.

"Are you sure I shouldn't just zap him?" Dandy whispered.

Malcolm nudged him. "He's too fast."

Bailey tugged the reins and the horse pranced forward.

Malcolm gulped, hoping the phantom couldn't see his quivering hands. "Here you go," he said, tacking on the brightest smile he could manage. He carefully handed the head over to the horseman.

Bailey held it out, considering it. Then to their delight, he plopped it right on top of his shoulders.

It took every ounce of willpower to keep Malcolm from laughing out loud. It was a sight. Bailey's bulky, masculine frame was now topped off by a milky-white wig head with a bad perm.

"You look fantastic!" Malcolm lied. "Doesn't he look great?" he said to Dandy.

Dandy's cheeks puffed out like he was holding in an oversized chuckle. He drew a deep breath and said, "He could be on the cover of Handsome Horseman magazine."

Malcolm waited, hoping Bailey would accept the new head and ride off into the sunset.

But Bailey had another plan. He stood up on his horse, poising his arms over his head. Then lifting up on his tippy-toes, he twirled round and round. The perfect ballerina.

Malcolm nudged Dandy. "Are you seeing what I'm seeing?"

"Are you seeing a body spinning faster than a head?" Dandy asked.

"Uh, yeah."

Bailey's pirouettes were spot on, but as his body circled, the Styrofoam head sat still and wobbly.

"I have a bad feeling about this," Malcolm said.

In a matter of moments, Bailey's new head tilted a tad too far. It popped off his shoulders and landed in the grass, right in front of his horse. The horse let out an eerie *neigh-hay-hay* and took a huge bite out of it.

Malcolm and Dandy shared a look. How is it possible that a horsey apparition could munch down on a Styrofoam head? They watched as the horse chewed it up, then spit out the wig.

Malcolm leaned toward Dandy. "Oops!"

Dandy was already inching backward. "So what do we do now?"

Bailey pulled on the reins and the horse reared back.

"Run!" Malcolm cried.

They hauled forward, arms flailing.

"I don't think we can outrun him!" Dandy huffed.

The horse and rider were upon them. They were so close Malcolm could feel the horse's snorting breath on his neck. But just as Bailey was about to trample them, Malcolm and Dandy made it to the barn. They kicked open the door and tumbled into a mound of hay.

"Did we shake him?" Dandy asked, spitting some straw out of his mouth.

Malcolm looked over at the stable door. No ghost. "I think it's safe for now."

Malcolm stood up and brushed off some hay poking out of his hair. Then he heard *neigh-hay-hay-hay-hay*. Lulu had Dandy pinned against a stall, licking his face with big, wet, horsey kisses.

Strike!

"**I**'ve got it!" Dandy said, rushing through the door the next morning. He was lugging a green and silver bag with the words *Born to Roll* written on the front.

"What's that?" Malcolm asked.

Dandy dropped it on the floor with a major *thud!* "It's my dad's bowling ball."

"Won't your dad be mad if we give it away?"

Dandy unzipped the bag and, using both hands, heaved the ball out. It was tomato red with smoky gray swirls. "It's okay. Dad hasn't been bowling since his hand got stuck in the finger holes and he slid into the gutter."

"Ouch!" Malcolm said, glad that Mr. Dee hadn't gotten caught in the pin machine. Or had he? "But think about it," he told Dandy. "It's going to hurt a lot if Bailey hurls this head at us. I don't want to be a human bowling pin."

"It's too heavy to throw," Dandy said. "Besides, he'll like it." He turned the ball around to the holes. "It's got a cute face. See?"

Those finger holes did look a lot like two eyes and a mouth. "It looks scared, like it's seen a ghost," Malcolm pointed out.

"You think he'll like it?" Dandy asked.

An idea flashed through Malcolm's genius brain. He took the ball from Dandy and dropped it into the bag. "He doesn't have to like it. He just has to be curious."

Malcolm hooked the bowling bag to his bike instead of Dandy's. Dandy had enough problems pedaling without feeling like he was pumping a fourteen-pound schnauzer on his handlebars. It was a miracle he'd gotten it here to begin with.

"So what's the new plan?" Dandy asked as they rounded into the stables.

"We'll roll it to him this time," Malcolm answered. "He'll have to get off the horse to pick it up."

Dandy stumbled off his bike. "And?"

"And then we zap him," Malcolm whispered in case Bailey was lurking nearby.

There was no sign of Mr. Gable, but that wasn't surprising. He was petrified of Bailey. And now Malcolm knew why.

The horses were out grazing, munching the stalks of tall grass.

"Uh-oh," Dandy said, slipping behind Malcolm. "Don't let her see me."

Malcolm was busy gathering the tools. "Who?"

Dandy pointed to Lulu, who was chewing a long, golden reed. "Her."

"We've got bigger things to worry about," Malcolm said. "Here." He handed the specter detector over to Dandy. "I'll man the zapper."

It didn't take long for Bailey to make an appearance. He strode up to them, paused, then cracked his knuckles.

That's not good, Malcolm thought. "Hey, Bailey," he said, holding up the bowling ball. "Brought you another head."

Bailey flexed his fingers, then pounded one fist into the other.

"He doesn't seem too happy," Dandy whispered.

"This will cheer him up," Malcolm said. He rolled the bowling ball right up to the horse's phantom hooves. "There. Try it on."

Bailey hesitated, scratching his shoulder.

"Looks like he's mulling it over," Malcolm whispered to Dandy.

Dandy took a quick step back. "As long as he doesn't mull us over."

Then Bailey did exactly what they were hoping. He climbed off his horse and reached for the ball.

"Now!" Dandy yelled.

Malcolm hit the button on the zapper. But Bailey bent down at that exact moment, and the zapper foam shot right

over him, hitting the horse! And with a gurgled *neigh-hay-hay*, the horse became a giant puddle, soaking into the ground.

"You missed!" Dandy cried.

Malcolm couldn't believe it. How could he have missed? But he didn't have time to worry about that now because Bailey had snatched up the ball and plopped it on his shoulders.

Uh oh!

Bailey now had a tomato-red acrylic head with a face that had gone from scared to scary. And he was stomping their way.

"Uh, Dandy," Malcolm stuttered.

Dandy was already backing up. "I know. *Run!*"

Wipe Out!

Malcolm and Dandy shot off, racing across the field.

"Is he behind us?" Dandy huffed, his arms pumping like a locomotive.

Malcolm didn't have to look back to know that Bailey was just a step or two behind. "Keep moving!"

A few times he saw Bailey's arm reaching dangerously close. But they managed to propel forward before getting snatched.

"Man, he's fast," Dandy said.

"Yeah, lucky for us he has a fourteen-pound bowling ball for a head. If that wasn't weighing him down we'd be toast."

They cut left, heading toward the barn.

"Think we'll be safe again in there?" Dandy asked.

Malcolm doubted it. If Bailey was willing to chase them down on foot, he meant business.

Then Malcolm spotted a miracle. The one thing that could help them ditch Bailey and his fat tomato head.

"Over there!" he shouted, pointing to the fence.

"Are you kidding?" Dandy yelled, his knees bobbing as he sprinted.

"Nope," Malcolm answered. "Your girlfriend's waiting."

They charged ahead, hopped onto the fence rail, then – *whumph!* – landed on Lulu's back.

Malcolm leaned forward and wrapped his arms around Lulu's neck, careful not to drop the zapper. "Hang on."

"I'm trying!" Dandy cried, clinging to Malcolm's shirt.

Lulu tramped ahead. After putting some distance between them and Bailey, she slowed to a trot. Malcolm and Dandy bounced like a paddleball.

"Whoa," Malcolm called, trying to bring Lulu to a complete stop.

Dandy relaxed his grip on Malcolm's shirt. "That was close. Did you see how fast Bailey ran? He could win a medal."

Malcolm grinned. "For running or bowling?"

Dandy chuckled. "You think we've lost him?"

Malcolm looked back and saw Bailey was cycling toward them on Dandy's bike.

"Not fair!" Dandy yelled. "He can reach the pedals."

"And he's fast," Malcolm added. "Giddy-up!"

Lulu kicked into a full gallop, knocking the boys against each other. They wobbled but soon were upright and balanced.

Malcolm lightly spurred Lulu's sides, urging her on. "What's going on back there?" he asked Dandy.

Dandy twisted for a better look. "Uh, you won't believe it."

Malcolm turned too. Dandy was right. It was unbelievable. Bailey was standing up on the bike, knees bent and arms out, surfer style.

"Wow, he's good," Dandy said.

"Yeah," Malcolm agreed. "He really should've been in the circus."

"I can't believe the bike is pedaling itself," Dandy added.

"Through tall grass!" Malcolm said.

Malcolm tapped Lulu's shanks with his feet again, urging her on. She wasn't exactly a racehorse, but she could gallop like the wind.

"Are we losing him?" Malcolm asked, hanging on for dear life. He ventured a look back. Bailey was right behind them, reaching out for Lulu's tail.

"Is there a jet engine on that bike?" Malcolm asked.

"Not when I'm riding it," Dandy said. "Maybe it's being propelled by ghost power."

"Whatever it is, we need to find a way to stop it." Malcolm looked back again. Bailey's fingers were still close to Lulu's tail.

But that wasn't their only problem. Just ahead was an empty hay cart, unhitched and tilted to the ground. Lulu was heading right for it.

Malcolm didn't know how to steer her away. He was clinging to her neck and the zapper. If only he had a few extra hands.

He wasn't sure what would be worse, crashing into the hay cart or being smashed in the skull with Bailey's new head.

"Malcolm!" Dandy cried, observing the situation. "Uh . . . Malcolm!"

"I know! I know! What are we going to do?" Malcolm cried.

Lulu made that decision for them. Just as Bailey was about to grasp a handful of her tail, she cut to the right. That's when Bailey saw the hay cart—much too late! The

bike rode up it like a ramp and slammed into the rails, sending Bailey flying high into the air. He did two somersaults, then landed with both feet on the ground.

He stood for a moment, sort of dizzy. But that moment was all Malcolm needed. He pressed the button of the zapper, spraying Bailey with zapper juice. He instantly evaporated, leaving the bowling ball suspended for half a second. Then – *thump!* – it plopped down into the puddle.

"Got him!" Dandy said.

Lulu grinned with her big, horsey teeth. *Neigh-hay-hay.*

"Great job," Mr. Gable said as he helped Dandy untangle his bike from the railings of the cart. "I won't be bothered by that headless clown again."

Dandy unhooked the handlebars and pulled his bike free. The front wheel was bent, and the seat had pushed down. Dandy straddled it. "Hey! I can reach the pedals now."

Mr. Gable scratched his head. "You could've reached them all along if you'd just used a screwdriver to lower the seat."

Dandy sighed.

Malcolm patted Lulu's neck. "Guess we're done here," he said.

"I can't let you boys leave without a little reward," Mr. Gable said.

Malcolm and Dandy shared a bright look. How much cash was Mr. Gable about to lay on them?

"Since I'm so grateful," Mr. Gable began, "I want you boys to stop by and ride Lulu any time you want. No charge."

Malcolm and Dandy shared a not-so-bright look. Malcolm's bottom was still sore from bouncing around on Lulu's back.

"Thanks," he said. "That's really nice of you."

Malcolm and Dandy gathered up the tools. "What about the bowling ball?" Malcolm asked. "Don't you want to bring it back to your dad?"

"No way," Dandy answered. "It's covered in ghost goo. Bleck."

"Yeah," Malcolm agreed. "His fingers would stick for sure."

They hopped on their bikes and were about to leave when – *neigh-hay-hay* – Lulu trotted up behind them. She plodded right up to Dandy and – *slurrrrppp!* – gave him a big, wet kiss.

Malcolm smiled. "Your girlfriend is going to miss you."

"She's not my girlfriend!"

Dandy wiped the horse slobber from his cheek. Then, they pedaled away from Mr. Gable's haunt-free stables.

TOOLS OF THE TRADE
FIVE USES FOR THE GHOST HUNTER'S BIKE

From Ghost Detectors Malcolm and Dandy

1. Use it for transportation to find spirits.

2. Tell your parents you are out riding on it for exercise so you can get out of the house for the afternoon to hunt ghosts.

3. Loan it to your best friend so he or she can get away from evil specters.

4. Attach a basket and use it to haul your ghost-detecting tools.

5. Let an angry spirit chase you with your bike so it can ride up a ramp and fall, giving you enough time to zap it!